This book belongs to.

....

....

27 Longford Street, London NW1 3DZ

Printed in Belgium

I Can Read a Rainbow

Written and illustrated by

Rene Cloke

AWARD PUBLICATIONS LIMITED

THE LITTLE HOUSE WITH THE RED DOOR

"This is becoming a nuisance," said Cranberry, "the wind has blown down my house three times this week," and he looked at the scattered twigs that had once been a snug squirrel's drey. "I shall build a strong house on the ground," he decided, and began to collect all sorts of things which looked as though they *couldn't* be blown over.

Then he planned out the number of rooms he would want; a sitting-room, a bedroom and a kitchen. He hammered sticks into the ground and piled up stones for the walls, he stuck moss and mud into all the holes and made a nice little window for each room. It looked rather queer but it was strong.

"Now I'll thatch the roof," said Cranberry, "and my house will be finished."

Then it really did look like a house and Cranberry called his rabbit friend, Bouncer, to come and see it.

"Very nice," said Bouncer, "but how do you get in? There's no door."

Cranberry was horrified; he ran all around the house but Bouncer was right, he had forgotten to make a doorway.

"Of course, you could climb in and out of the windows," suggested Bouncer, "but it would look rather undignified."

Cranberry sat down in despair but Bouncer looked around. "I've got an idea," he cried. "See this hollow tree close to your house? We'll dig a tunnel from inside the tree to the inside of your house and you can put a door over the hollow trunk."

Bouncer was good at digging and between them they dug a tunnel inside the tree and came up in the middle of Cranberry's house. Then they made a little door, fixed it over the hollow, and painted it red to match the windowsills.

"It's the most beautiful house I've ever seen," declared Cranberry and he and Bouncer went along the tunnel into the house and ate an enormous tea.

THE RUNAWAY ORANGE

Mrs Prettyone was doing her shopping. She had nearly filled her basket and was wondering whether to buy bananas or apples when she saw the oranges.

"Very nice and juicy," said Mr Spinach, "I can recommend them."

"I'll take four," decided Mrs Prettyone. "One for me, one for Dad, one for Poppet and one for Pickles – no, I'll take five, one for old Mrs Plumtree, I'm sure she would enjoy one."

Mrs Prettyone left the shop with the bag of oranges balanced on the top of her basket but, as she started walking down the hill, the bag slipped and the top orange jumped out.

"Catch it, catch it!" she called to old Mr Hobble who was passing by, but Mr Hobble just looked at the bouncing orange and walked on.

"Never did like oranges," he mumbled. The orange rolled on and Mrs Prettyone sped after it.

"Stop that orange!" she cried to a rabbit who sat in front of her burrow.

"Nasty slippery things," answered the rabbit, pushing it aside, "I don't want it in *my* burrow!"

"Oh, please stop that orange!" Mrs Prettyone cried to a pair of young badgers, but the badgers thought that the orange was a ball to play with and kicked it to and fro until it bounced off down the hill again.

It was no good calling to a frightened little mouse who came out of the hedge; she was so terrified of being knocked over that she scuttled for shelter until the orange had rolled past.

"Oh dear!" gasped Mrs Prettyone, as she panted on. "I can't possibly catch it and old Mrs Plumtree will never have her orange now."

Peter Pixie did try to stop it but missed it.

"Just as well," said Mrs Prettyone, "I'm sure he would have eaten it himself." And then she stopped and burst out laughing. The orange had taken a bounce and a jump and landed on the doorstep of Mrs Plumtree's cottage, where the old lady was sitting in the sun.

"Oh, what a lovely present," Mrs Plumtree cried, "and how clever of you to roll it all the way to my cottage!"

THE YELLOW DRAGON

Dusty was a town mouse and he had never seen any trees or flowers until he spent a holiday with Russet, the harvest mouse.

"While I tidy the house," said Russet after breakfast, "you can go for a walk. The fresh air will put some colour into your pale grey cheeks."

Dusty stepped out into the sunshine and wandered down the lane.

"What strange, brightly coloured things," he murmured, staring at the honeysuckle and the poppies. "What can they be?"

A butterfly fluttered by and Dusty hid behind a stone in alarm. "It's very beautiful," he said. "I wonder if it's dangerous?"

He walked on nervously and then he saw something that nearly made him jump out of his grey skin.

"Why it's a dragon!" he gasped. "It must be a dragon!" and he turned and ran back, helter-skelter, to Russet's house.

"Help, help!" he yelled, "there's a dragon in the lane – a yellow dragon! I only saw its head but it opened and closed its mouth in a most frightening way when I looked at it!"

"Rubbish," laughed Russet, "there are no dragons here. You've been dreaming!"

"Oh, do come,' cried Dusty, "you must come and see it. It's quite a small dragon but it looks so fierce!"

So Russet took Dusty's paw and they walked down the lane together.

"There," whispered Dusty, pointing at the hedge. "Look, there it is!"

Russet threw back his head and laughed.

"Why, that's a flower," he said, "a yellow toadflax. And look, Dick Dormouse is hiding behind it and pressing it so that it looks like a mouth opening and shutting!"

Dusty looked closely and there was the little dormouse with a paw on each side of the flower; and as he pressed it, it looked just like a hungry dragon opening and shutting its mouth. Russet nibbled through the stem and gave the toadflax to Dusty.

"You shall take it home with you," he said, "and show your friends how dangerous it is to live in the country!"

THE GREEN UMBRELLA

Dandy suddenly remembered that it was Guy Fawkes Day tomorrow. "I'll run along to Mrs Honeypot's shop and buy as many fireworks as I can to let off on the village green," he decided. It was a wet morning so he took his big green umbrella as well as his shopping basket.

First he bought a loaf of bread, some sausages and a packet of biscuits, then he went to Mrs Honeypot's shop. There were some fine big rockets, Catherine wheels, squibs and Roman candles for sale and Dandy chose twelve of the very best ones.

"I'll put them in a bag for you," said Mrs Honeypot, "your basket's full all ready."

It had stopped raining and Dandy walked home feeling very pleased with himself but, when he looked for his fireworks the next evening, he couldn't find them anywhere.

"I didn't put them in my basket, there wasn't room, and I know I had the bag in my hand when I left the shop because Mrs Honeypot had to open the door for me."

He looked in all the cupboards and in every drawer in the house; he even looked in the dustbin although he was quite sure they weren't there. Then he sat down and thought and thought.

Bang! Pop! Pop! Everyone else was letting off fireworks on the village green so Dandy went out to join them.

"It won't be much fun now I haven't any of my own," he sighed.

"O-o-oh!" A beautiful Catherine wheel spun round and round. "Ah-ah-a-a!" A shower of green stars came falling from the sky. Dandy gave a gasp. "It looks just like my green umbrella," he said. "Why – of course!" and he dashed back to his house.

There, inside the umbrella, were the missing fireworks – he remembered that the bag had burst and, as the rain had stopped, he had emptied the fireworks into his umbrella.

Whizz! Bang! Pop-pop! Off went Dandy's fireworks and they were quite the best that anyone had ever seen.

THE BLUE SHOES THAT WALKED BY THEMSELVES

"I think I shall wear my blue shoes this afternoon," said Pipkin. "No, perhaps not, the brown ones will be better for a country walk."

He put on his brown shoes and walked out of his cottage. The blue shoes were furious. They peeped round the open door and watched Pipkin's feet, in the brown shoes, skipping down the lane.

"Let's go out by ourselves," said Left Shoe.

"Do you think we could?" asked Right Shoe.

"Of course," answered Left, "I'm not going to wait for a foot inside me."

Off they went, feeling rather peculiar but managing quite well.

"I'm going down to the river," said Right.

"Well, I shall go into the forest," said Left. "Mind you get home before Pipkin."

Right had a lovely time by the river until he pretended to be a boat and then he got so wet that he sank to the bottom and had to be helped out by a water vole.

"I shall have to stay here and try to get dry," he whimpered as he shivered on the riverbank.

Left trotted into the forest and wandered about amongst the trees, talking to the rabbits and squirrels. He had fun playing hide-and-seek with them but got badly

scratched as he scrambled through the bramble bushes. Then he lost his way and it was quite dark when he and a very damp Right met on the doorstep.

They crept into the cottage and sat side by side by Pipkin's bed.

When Pipkin woke up the next morning he looked at them in surprise.

"I feel sure that I wore my brown shoes yesterday," he said, "but my blue shoes look wet and muddy!" He rubbed his head. "How bad my memory is getting!"

So he put on his brown shoes and the blue shoes were left at home for a second day.

"We won't go out by ourselves again," they decided, "or we'll never have our turn to go out properly with Pipkin."

And that evening they were given such a cleaning and polishing that they felt quite sore for hours and hours.

THE CAT IN THE INDIGO CAR

Honey, the ginger cat, was having a terrible morning; he couldn't make up his mind about anything.

He couldn't even decide what to have for breakfast and, as soon as he had cooked some porridge instead of bacon, he wondered if he would rather have had an egg.

Then he spent half an hour choosing which scarf he would wear before going out for an important piece of shopping, for he was going to buy a new car.

In the car showroom it was just as bad and he was so long making up his mind about the colour he liked that all the cars but the deep indigo blue one were sold.

"That's quite a relief," sighed Honey, "now I shan't have to choose," and he drove off happily to finish his shopping.

It took him the rest of the morning to decide between a tin of soup and a packet of sausages and then he thought he would rather have a pork pie instead.

Outside the shop he met his friend, Porky Puss, looking very sad. "I've lost my purse," sobbed Porky Puss, "I must have dropped it on the way here. I shall have to spend the rest of the day looking for it."

"I'll keep a look out for it," said Honey.

It grew colder and started to snow as Honey drove home.

"Perhaps I should have bought that tin of soup," he murmured, "it would have been more warming than the pie."

After lunch he went for a drive in his new car. Spinning merrily over the snowy road, he began wondering which way he would go when he reached the crossroads – left or right?

"Oh, I can't make up my mind," he sighed as he stood under the signpost and looked first in one direction, then the other. "I'll toss up."

He spun a penny into the air and when it fell to the ground it was half buried in the snow.

Honey dug it out and there, hidden by the snow-covered leaves, was Porky Puss's purse!

"What luck!" cried Honey. "If I hadn't been so undecided, I wouldn't have tossed up and if I hadn't tossed up, I wouldn't have found Porky Puss's purse! Now I shan't have to decide which way to go; I'll go straight to Porky Puss's house with the purse and be just in time for tea!"

VIOLET COTTAGE

"Summer is over," said Spindle, "so I must find a cosy place for my winter sleep," and she peeped into all the cottage gardens.

"Red Roofs, no, they have a dog and, although I can protect myself by rolling into a prickly ball, I won't go there."

There was a big cat at The Orange Tree and Spindle didn't like cats. Yellow Shutters had only a paved courtyard, "Too cold," she shuddered.

The trees at Green Gates were evergreens and Spindle wanted dry dead leaves for a snug bed.

The pond in the middle of the lawn at The Blue Lagoon made her shiver.

"How dreadful if I fell in on a dark night!" she thought.

The indigo blue car in the drive of the next cottage also looked dangerous but, at last, Spindle found just what she wanted.

Violet Cottage had violet curtains and an old lady with violet ribbon on her cap sat in the window.

Spindle crept around to the garden shed and snuggled down amongst a heap of dead leaves.

"I shall look forward to the violets in flower in the spring," she murmured as she fell asleep.

The hedgehog spent a cosy night in the shed and the next morning she decided to go into the garden and have a good meal before settling down for her long winter sleep.

She wandered about all day enjoying the autumn sunshine and having a chat with a friendly robin. But when the sun went down and the air became cooler she made her way back to the shed. "How snug my bed of dry leaves will be," she said as she trotted along.

But the door of the shed was bolted! "What shall I do?" whimpered the little hedgehog. "I shall have to start looking all over again for a bed for the winter."

"Hallo!" barked a deep voice. "What's the matter?" There stood Ruff, the big dog from Red Roofs.

The little hedgehog forgot all about being frightened of dogs. "The shed door is bolted and I can't get in to my bed of dry leaves for the winter," she said.

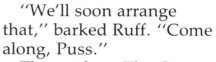

"We'll soon arrange that," barked Ruff. "Come along, Puss."

The cat from The Orange Tree sprang over the fence and jumped on to the dog's back. Then, with her clever little paws, she pushed back the bolt and opened the door.

"Thank you! Thank you!" said the hedgehog as she scuttled into the shed. Ruff shut the door and Puss bolted it.

"Sleep well until the spring!" they cried. "Goodnight."